The Nutcracker Ballet

Based on the story by E.T.A. Hoffman

Retold by Carol Thompson • Illustrated by Darcy May

Cartwheel
B·O·O·K·S ®

SCHOLASTIC INC.

New York Toronto London Auckland Sydney

ISBN 0-590-48197-5

Text copyright © 1994 by Scholastic Inc.
Illustrations copyright © 1994 by Darcy May.
All rights reserved. Published by Scholastic Inc.
CARTWHEEL BOOKS is a registered trademark of Scholastic Inc.

12 11 10 9 8 7 6 5 4 3 2 1   4 5 6 7 8 9/9

Printed in the U.S.A.   24

First Scholastic printing, October 1994

It was Christmas Eve. Marie and Fritz could hardly wait for the Christmas party to begin!

Behind the closed doors of the living room, their parents were decorating for the party. Marie peeked through the keyhole, trying to catch a glimpse of the Christmas tree.

Soon the guests arrived, and the big doors were opened wide. There in the middle of the room stood the most beautiful tree Marie and Fritz had ever seen!

It sparkled with the light of a hundred candles. Toys, cookies, and candy canes hung from the branches. Underneath the tree were colorful gifts of all shapes and sizes, and a golden star was shining brightly at the top.

Godfather Drosselmeyer walked into the room, and
the guests began to whisper excitedly. Drosselmeyer was
a famous toymaker. His toys seemed almost magical!

Some of the children were afraid of Drosselmeyer,
with his wild white hair and his black eye patch.
But Marie loved him dearly.

Drosselmeyer brought in two big boxes. All the guests gathered around to see what wonderful toys he had made. Slowly, he opened the green box. A toy ballerina leapt out and started to dance!

Then Drosselmeyer untied the red ribbon, and a big toy soldier kicked open the box and began marching. Everyone clapped and cheered.

Drosselmeyer gave his goddaughter a special present.
It was a wooden nutcracker shaped like a little soldier.

Naughty Fritz snatched the nutcracker away
and stuffed a big walnut into its mouth.
CRACK! CRACK! CRACK! Three teeth fell out!

"Stop it, Fritz!" Marie cried.
"It's an ugly thing," said Fritz, "and it
doesn't even work!"

Marie took the nutcracker away from Fritz and hugged it tightly. "Never mind," she whispered to the nutcracker. "I'll always take care of you."

Drosselmeyer helped Marie tie a handkerchief around the nutcracker's jaw. "Don't worry," he said. "Your nutcracker will be all right after a good night's rest."

Soon the party was over and the children went off to bed.

But Marie couldn't sleep. She crept downstairs to see her nutcracker one more time. On the floor beside his little bed, she fell fast asleep. Marie didn't see Godfather Drosselmeyer come into the room and fix the nutcracker's jaw.

The clock chimed midnight. Marie woke with a start, not knowing where she was. She looked around the dark room and realized that everything around her was growing bigger!

The Christmas tree towered above her. The toys under the tree were nearly her size, and so was the nutcracker!

Suddenly Marie heard the sound of footsteps.
She turned and saw an army of huge mice charging
toward the toys!

The nutcracker drew his sword and led the toy soldiers into battle. The other toys followed, and soon teddy bears, dolls, and puppets all had joined in the fight against the mice.

Something whizzed past Marie's head. The dolls were firing gumdrops from the toy cannon!

The toys fought hard, but there were too many mice. Then the King of the Mice knocked the nutcracker down. With an evil laugh, he raised his sword above the nutcracker's head.

Oh, no! thought Marie. *I must do something!* She took off her slipper and threw it at the Mouse King. The shoe hit his head and knocked him off balance.

The nutcracker quickly jumped up and attacked the king. In the wink of an eye, the Mouse King was dead, and the battle was over!

The nutcracker took the Mouse King's crown so he could give it to Marie. But Marie was lying on the bed. She had fainted from all the excitement!

The nutcracker climbed onto the bed and stood at the head, as if he were captain of a sailing ship. He pointed his sword at the window, and it swung open. Then the bed sailed away, across the starry sky.

Soon the bed came to rest in a snowy woods. Marie awoke and saw that her nutcracker had changed into a handsome prince.

He smiled at her and said, "My dear Marie, thank you for helping me win the battle. Now let me take you to my kingdom, the Land of Sweets."

The Nutcracker Prince took Marie's hand and led her through the woods to his palace. The beautiful Sugar Plum Fairy was waiting at the gate to meet them.

The Sugar Plum Fairy showed Marie and the Nutcracker Prince into a sparkling crystal hall where they sat upon a huge golden throne.

"Let the festivities begin!" said the Sugar Plum Fairy. All the happy people of the Land of Sweets came to dance in honor of the prince's return.

First a beautifully dressed couple did the dance of hot chocolate. Then came the dance of coffee, with a dancer who twirled and leapt high into the air.

A pair in silken costumes from China jumped out
of an enormous teapot to perform the dance of tea.

Mother Ginger swept into the hall wearing a
large hoopskirt which hid a surprise — a band of
mischievous children who did a merry dance!

At last the flowers of the land came to perform a lovely waltz. Their swirling colors and sweet perfume made Marie dizzy with happiness.

"What a beautiful place this is," sighed Marie. "Promise you'll bring me back here someday."

"You can always visit in your dreams," said the Nutcracker Prince with a smile.

All too soon, it was time for Marie to go home.
She and the prince stepped into his magic sleigh and
waved farewell.

"Good-bye! Good luck!" called the people of the
Land of Sweets as the sleigh carried Marie and the
prince high above the clouds.

The next morning, Marie woke up and found the nutcracker in her arms.

"You're as good as new!" she exclaimed. "Just as Godfather Drosselmeyer said you would be!"

Marie smiled and hugged her precious nutcracker, thinking of her wonderful night in the Land of Sweets. Had her adventure been only a dream...or just a bit of Christmas magic?